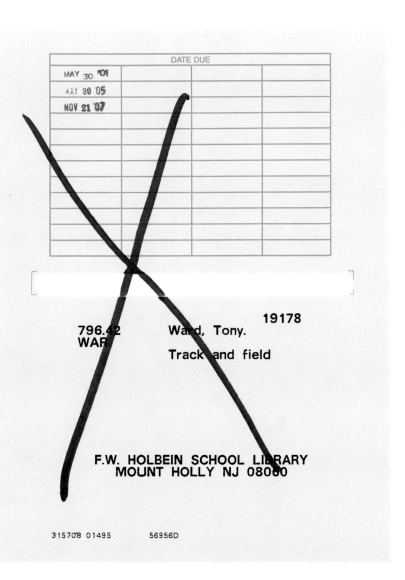

TRACK AND FIELD

Tony Ward

RIGBY
INTERACTIVE
LIBRARY

Produced by Mandarin Offset Ltd., Hong Kong
Printed in China
Designed by Ron Kamen, Green Door Design
Illustrated by Barry Atkinson

02 01 00 99 98
10 9 8 7 6 5 4 3 2 1

Ward, Tony, 1931-
    Track and field / Tony Ward.
        p.   cm. – (Successful sports)
    Includes index.
    Summary: Briefly describes the equipment, skills, tactics, and rules involved in track and field competition.
    ISBN 1-57572-201-1 (lib. bdg.)
    1. Track-athletics – Juvenile literature. [1. Track and field.] I. Title. II. Series.
GV1060.5.W264 1997
796.42 – dc21   96-52603
                                                                                     CIP
                                                                                     AC

Acknowledgments
The publisher would like to thank the following for permission to reproduce photographs: Allsport: pp. 5, 13, 15, 16, 19, 20, 22, 25, 27, 28, 29; Colorsport: title page and p. 24; Empics: pp. 23, 26; Sporting Pictures: pp. 9, 12; Mike Liles: p. 14; Meg Sullivan: pp. 4, 8, 10, 11, 18, 21. All other photographs supplied by the Author. Cover photograph © Empics.

The cover photo shows Michael Johnson winning the 200 meters at the 1996 Olympic Games in Atlanta. He was the first man in Olympic history to win both the 200 meters and the 400 meters. The title page photo shows Roger Black anchoring the Great Britain 4 by 400-meters relay team to success in the 1994 World Cup at Crystal Palace.

The publishers and author would like to thank the Run, Jump, Throw club run by Maureen Jones, Steve Buchanan, and Keeth Elementary School for their help with the photographs.

Note to the Reader
Some words in this book are printed in bold type. This indicates that the word is listed in the glossary on page 30. The glossary gives a brief explanation of words that may be new to you.

Contents

The Birth of Track and Field

People have run races against one another as a sport for thousands of years. As long ago as about 700 B.C., the Greek poet Homer told the story of a famous foot race. The first organized track and field **meets** took place in ancient Greece as part of the **Olympic Games**. The Games included running and jumping competitions and throwing the discus and the javelin. Later there was also a five-event competition called the **pentathlon**. These early Games were stopped in 393 A.D. because of cheating and other dishonest behavior. In the mid-1800s, in Europe, track and field as a sport started again in schools and universities. After visiting interested athletes in Britain, the Frenchman Baron Pierre de Coubertin restarted the Olympic Games. The first modern Olympics, including many of the well-known track and field events, took place in Athens, Greece in 1896. Apart from the world war years, the Olympic Games have been held every four years since then. Track and field events have always been major Olympic sports. Women's track and field entered the Olympics in 1928.

The glittering opening ceremony at the 1992 Olympic Games in Barcelona, Spain.

Safety first

Warming-up and cooling-down are very important to keep you injury free. Exercise or jogging before training or competing can do the trick. Jogging slowly for a few minutes afterwards is equally vital.

Equipment

Getting started in track and field is not expensive. The most important equipment a beginner needs in any of the events is a good pair of athletic shoes. Athletic shoes should fit comfortably and protect the feet from injury. If you decide to take up a track and field event seriously, then you may need spiked shoes. The only clothing required are t-shirts and shorts, and a sweatsuit for keeping warm. For those taking up field events such as javelin, discus, and shot put, schools and local organizations usually provide beginners with suitable equipment.

Many young people get interested in track and field at school. To improve your skills and have a chance to enter competitions, you may want to join a local club. Clubs can give advice as well as opportunities for extra training. Before joining a club, find out as much as possible about it. Make sure that there are experienced coaches, regular entries by club members into competitions, well-equipped **facilities**, and a helpful atmosphere. Having fun and not specializing too early are keys to enjoying track and field. International athletes often say they'll retire when the enjoyment goes.

To see if you would like to start training in a track and field event, you can take part in the Junior Olympics run by the U.S.A. Track and Field Federation and the Amateur Athletic Union locally and nationally.

Stadiums, Surfaces, and Safety

Track and field offers the greatest variety of any sport. The two main divisions are the field events and the track events. Field events usually take place on the field in the center of the **stadium** and include javelin, shot put, discus, hammer, triple jump, pole vault, high jump, and long jump. The track events are all those that include running and hurdling, and these usually take place on a track that circles the field. The two exceptions are the marathon and walking events. Usually these events take place outside of the stadium.

The running tracks and runways are usually made of a **synthetic** material, and the throwing surface take-off areas are concrete. Before the 1950s, tracks were made of **cinder**. The first Olympics held on a synthetic surface were at Mexico City in 1968, and today this type of surface has become the most common. A major outdoor stadium has an eight-lane, 400-meter running track. It also has a long **straight** for the **sprints** and hurdles races. Because of the problems wind can cause, a big stadium might have runways and landing areas at both ends, as well as javelin runways and throwing circles at each end of the stadium. This ensures the safety of the athletes, officials, and spectators.

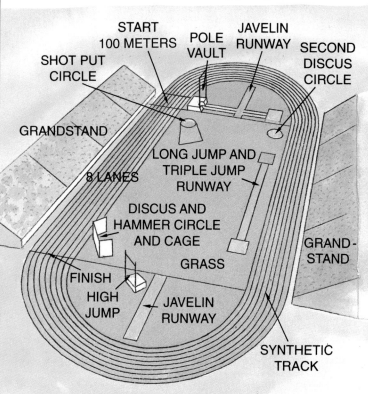

START 100 METERS
POLE VAULT
JAVELIN RUNWAY
SECOND DISCUS CIRCLE
SHOT PUT CIRCLE
GRANDSTAND
LONG JUMP AND TRIPLE JUMP RUNWAY
8 LANES
DISCUS AND HAMMER CIRCLE AND CAGE
GRASS
GRAND-STAND
FINISH
HIGH JUMP
JAVELIN RUNWAY
SYNTHETIC TRACK

Layout of a typical stadium.

At school and most local club track meets, starting, timekeeping, and scoring are still done by hand. However, the most up-to-date electronic and computer-assisted methods are now used at the national and international level and at many local events. For example, the long jump and triple jump are measured by a modern device that does not require a tape measure, and the results are produced by a computer.

The famous Olympic Stadium in Munich was the site of the 1972 Olympic Games.

Because the throwing **implements** used in field events can be very dangerous, it is important that athletes follow safety rules very strictly when training and competing. For example, in training, group throwing often takes place. It is very important that all the throws are completed before the implements are collected from their landing places. Spectators must stand well behind the throwers and should be alert at all times. No throwing should ever take place without a teacher or a coach in charge.

Safety first

At all times, especially during training sessions, athletes should pay attention to coaches and officials and be aware of what is going on around them.

Safety is also important in the jumping events. The landing pits for the high jump and the pole vault should be made of high-quality foam, and in the long and triple jump, the sand in the pits should be thick enough and well-raked.

Running is the Key

Learning to run fast is an important skill in all athletic events. It is at the core of all other **techniques**. In events like the marathon and the 100 meters, it is obvious that running skills are vital. Speed and quickness are also basic skills needed in all the track and field events, from the triple jump to shot putting.

All jumpers and throwers need to learn special techniques for their events. A good technique will make the most of their approach to the height they are jumping or the distance they are throwing. However, a good specialist technique is not helpful unless it is combined with speed and power. This is what good running skills can bring to the athlete. No energy should be wasted on unnecessary action, and all movement must be directed forward. Shoulders, arms, and legs must work together. The eyes must be directed straight ahead and the head kept upright.

Speed on the runway is essential for all good long-jumpers.

American Carl Lewis and Heike Dreschler of Germany are two great long-jumpers who are also champion runners. They excel in the short distances, or sprints. Kim Batten of the United States set a world record for the 400-meters hurdles in 1995. Even while carrying a fiberglass pole, Sergei Bubka, the Ukrainian world record holder for the pole vault, could match most young sprinters running 40 meters. All these top athletes have realized the importance of speed running and have benefited from being fast.

Another skill that all athletes need to develop, not only those involved in athletics, is how to avoid **tension**. Tension tightens the muscles and slows movement. Over the last ten or twenty meters of a sprint race you can see the runners stiffen, or "tie up," as the tension overcomes them. To fight tension you need to be fit, relaxed, and confident. Keeping relaxed throughout a race right up to the end is one of the greatest skills of most successful runners. Watch Carl Lewis in a television slow-motion replay of a 100-meters race. From start to finish, he is perfectly relaxed. His muscles ripple and his cheeks wobble like jelly. Years of training and preparation have taught him how to relax his mind and body.

TRACK AND FIELD FACTS

American Carl Lewis has excelled as an all-around athlete because of his speed. At the World Championships in the ten years from 1983 to 1993, he won gold medals in three 100 meters, two long jumps, and three relay races.

Linford Christie of Great Britain is relaxed at top speed as he wins the 1993 world 100-meter title in Stuttgart.

Sprinting and Middle-distance and Distance Running

Running is the most popular of all track and field events, and everyone, from children to senior citizens, can participate. At the top levels of the sport, the fastest men travel 100 meters at 22.84 mph, and the fastest women can do the same distance at 21.35 mph. The best marathon runners cover the 26.2-mile course at 12.42 mph. The speeds for the distances in between vary, but each requires different techniques and training.

Sprinters cross the finish line. It is essential to think about sprinting through and well beyond the finish.

Sprinting

The distances for sprint competition are 100, 200, and 400 meters. At each distance the athlete attempts to maintain maximum speed for the longest period of time. In all sprint races it is the athlete who turns up his or her speed a notch at the end of the race who wins.

A fast start is vital in sprinting, especially at 100 meters. Because of this, starting practice is very important. The three commands are: "On your marks," "Set," and then the firing of the gun for the start. If one of the runners moves before the gun is fired, it is a known as a *false start*. Each runner is allowed one false start. A runner who makes two false starts in one race is **disqualified**.

In sprint racing, the start position used by the runners is called the **crouch start**. The runner kneels down on one knee with arms stretched out in front and the fingertips of both hands touching the track just behind the start line.

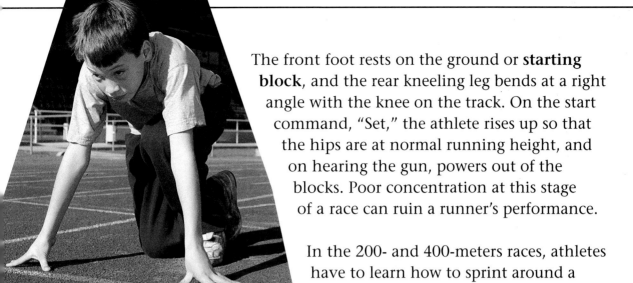

The front foot rests on the ground or **starting block**, and the rear kneeling leg bends at a right angle with the knee on the track. On the start command, "Set," the athlete rises up so that the hips are at normal running height, and on hearing the gun, powers out of the blocks. Poor concentration at this stage of a race can ruin a runner's performance.

In the 200- and 400-meters races, athletes have to learn how to sprint around a turn while staying in their lanes. The athletes are **staggered** in these races so that each will run an equal distance. For a longer sprint distance like the 400-meter, **pace judgment** is important. If the pace is too fast at the beginning, the runner is likely to run out of energy and slow down at the end of the race.

Middle-distance and distance
Middle-distance races of 800 and 1,500 meters require a good deal of **stamina** as well as speed. The greatest runners, such as the Moroccan Noureddine Morceli or the Russian Svetlana Masterkova, can hold records and win races at a variety of distances because of their staying power. Training and working on **tactics** are very important features of preparation for running the middle-distance races. Training ideas have changed over the years. Now most middle-distance runners practice on the track and do cross-country and road training.

The long-distance races run at track meets are the 5,000 and the 10,000 meters. For many years these distances have been the speciality of runners from the countries of East Africa. The most successful distance runners, like the famous Kip Keino, were born at high altitudes so their bodies can carry more oxygen in the blood. This is a great advantage in long-distance running. Also, many of the African runners had to travel long distances by foot to and from school every day—the perfect training for a future running career!

Hurdling and Steeplechasing

urdling is a track race run over obstacles. There are three hurdles races in track and field. Usually the shorter the race and the higher the hurdle, the more important good technique becomes. In hurdling, the distances run and the heights of the hurdles are different for men and women runners. Men run 110 meters over hurdles 42 inches high and women run 100 meters over 38-inch hurdles. High school races have shorter distances and lower hurdle heights because of the competitors' smaller size. A 400-meter race also has ten flights of hurdles for both men and women runners, but the men go over hurdles 36 inches high while the women go over 30-inch hurdles.

Sprint hurdlers run three strides between each of the ten hurdles. The good hurdler rises to the hurdle and then gets back onto the track into the normal sprinting position as quickly as possible. This is because time spent in the air is wasted in a hurdles race. A runner can gather speed only when in contact with the ground. The best hurdlers move their arms and legs around the hurdle, but keep their body in virtually the same position as when they are sprinting.

Watch a slow-motion replay of a good hurdler such as the American Roger Kingdom, and you can see how an expert does it. His head and body do not rise up from the running position as he crosses the hurdles.

The dominant
Kenyans
lead the
steeplechase
water-jump.

As his front (**leading**) leg goes up and over the hurdle, he leans forward to keep his balance and his back (**trailing**) leg curls sideways to clear the obstacle. To do this a hurdler has to be **limber**. Special training exercises help the body bend into these awkward positions.

The stride pattern when running between hurdles is very important in the 400-meter race, since the hurdles are farther apart. It is also a great advantage to be able to lead with either leg so you have the choice of taking an even number of strides between the obstacles. One of the best-ever hurdlers at this event is the British world record holder Sally Gunnell. As part of her race tactics, she regularly changes from fifteen to sixteen strides between hurdles at a particular point in the race because she can go over a hurdle with either leg first.

The steeplechase is run over 3,000 meters. It consists of 28 hurdles to be cleared as well as a water-jump with a log hurdle that the runners have to go over seven times. Today, only men run this race, but track and field event organizers plan to add it to the women's track events by the end of the century. The world's best steeplechasers, like the world's best long-distance runners, come from Kenya.

Jumping Basics

The four jumping events in field athletics are the high jump, the long jump, the triple jump, and the pole vault. The athletes competing in these four events try to achieve the greatest height or the longest length by using their own power combined with special techniques. The power that goes into a jump comes from the **approach run**.

In the long jump and the triple jump, an athlete's approach ends on a **take-off board**. The jumper must take off from exactly the right position on or behind the board or the jump is called a "fouled jump" and does not count. In the high jump and the pole vault, the position for take-off is not marked, but doing it at the best point is still important. If the take-off is good, the athlete will be at the highest position just as the bar is crossed. If the take-off is early or late, then the top of the curve of the jump will come before or after the bar is reached and it may be knocked off. Watch the athletes competing in the jumps. You will see them constantly practicing their run-ups to make sure they have them right.

It's important to get as much height off the board as is possible in the long jump.

TRACK AND FIELD FACTS

Currently, the only jumping events in which women can officially compete are the long jump, the high jump, and the triple jump.

Wind conditions in the stadium can affect run-ups as well as the jumps themselves. A head wind slows the jumper down while a tail wind will speed the jumper up. A tail wind of faster than two meters per second for either a long jump or a triple jump will make any records gained **invalid**.

Power training to gain strength and speed is important in good jumping. Many athletes do not do enough power training because they prefer to spend their time improving their techniques. Many years ago an American jumper told his British opponent how much he liked the man's technique, but how much more he liked his own heights! This is an important lesson. No matter how good your technique, no matter how good you look technically, you still need power. International jumpers and vaulters use weights to build muscle strength, especially in the legs. Younger athletes can benefit from bounding and jumping exercises. Even running up the stairs is good power training.

A jumper clears the bar with the Fosbury style in the high jump. Note the excellent arch of his body.

Jumping Events

All the jumping events at a track and field meet take place on the field, using specially prepared foam or sand landing pits. In the high jump and the pole vault, the goal is to jump as high as possible over a raised bar balanced horizontally across the top of two upright posts. In the long jump and the triple jump, the athletes try to jump as far as possible.

Michelle Griffiths gets good height in the triple jump.

The long jump

This event consists of a sprint run-up followed by a jump as far forward as possible, with the competitor landing in a sand-filled pit. A bad take-off can lead to a fouled attempt, while a bad landing can reduce the length measured. In most competitions, each athlete gets to make preliminary qualifying jumps and either three or six final jumps.

The triple jump

This was originally known as the hop, step, and jump, which describes the action of the competitor. The sprint approach is the same as the long jump, but the first two jumps take place on the runway area. The final jump starts at the end of the runway and finishes as far forward in the sand pit as possible. For the first two jumps the competitor takes off and lands on one foot, but on the final jump both feet land together in the pit. The distance is measured from the beginning of the first jump. Each athlete usually gets a certain number of preliminary attempts, and the top six or eight performers get three more attempts.

The high jump

Athletes are allowed to run toward the high jump from the large circular run-up area at any angle and can jump using any style they want. They must take off from one foot and must not knock the bar off. Jumpers are allowed three attempts at each height, and if they fail to clear the bar, then the highest they have already cleared counts as their best. Over the years competitors in this event have tried various ways of approach and jumping styles to get just that little bit higher. Probably the most well-known of these is the Fosbury flop. It is named after the U.S. jumper Dick Fosbury, who first used the technique in competition when he won the 1968 Olympic title. Instead of using one of the straddling styles in which one leg and then the other goes over, the jumper goes over head-first with the back arching over the bar. All top-class competitors now use a type of Fosbury flop.

A young athlete learns the Fosbury flop.

The pole vault

This is the only jumping event that requires any equipment: a long, thin fiberglass pole. Pole vaulters sprint down an approach runway while using both hands to hold the pole to one side at shoulder height. As they get near the pit, they stick one end of the pole down into a special box-shaped metal hole in the runway. Using the bending and springing action of the pole, vaulters launch into the air feet first, still holding onto the pole with both hands. As the pole straightens, they give one final twist and push with their hands against the pole for added height and then let go, propelling themselves over the bar. Pole vaulters get three attempts to cross the bar successfully at each height.

Throwing Basics

The throwing events in track and field are the shot put, the discus, the hammer, and the javelin. In all these events, the goal of the competitor is to throw the implement as far as possible without **fouling**. The competitor transfers speed to the implement by using the power of the throwing arm. This power is a combination of the strength of the athlete and the technique used in the lead-up to the throw.

Three of the four throwing events begin with the competitor standing in an area known as the "circle." It is inside the circle that the build-up of power must take place if the thrower is to be successful. In the discus and the hammer, the speed generated by the athlete rotating across the circle helps throw the implement a long distance. Shot putters build up speed and power by gliding forward across the circle. The transfer of speed and power to the implement occurs when the athlete stops and the implement continues to move.

The transfer of speed and power in javelin throwing is more like that in the jumping events because the athletes use a run-up. The throwing arm transfers the speed of the legs to the javelin when the athlete stops and throws.

A shot putter demonstrates the ideal position at the front of the circle. Young athletes practice a "standing put."

An athlete can increase his or her power through strength training. This can be done by weight training, in which the athlete gradually increases the weight of the objects lifted. In Greek mythology, Myron lifted a bull above his head every day from his birth, and his strength grew. Coaches don't recommend bull lifting, but weight training helps increase muscle bulk and strength. All weight training should be designed and supervised by experienced trainers.

Safety is clearly of great importance at throwing events. No one wants to be involved in an accident with a sailing hammer or javelin! Throwing areas are always roped off, and special high-fenced "cages" are built around the circle for the discus and hammer events at major meets. At school and club level, in training and at small competitions, everyone needs to pay attention to the special risks. High-school athletes do not compete in the hammer throw. Many high-school track and field associations do not have javelin events because of the danger of injury.

Yuri Syedykh of Russia, one of the greatest hammer throwers of all time, speeds across the circle.

Here are five rules that should always be followed when participating in throwing events:
1. Be alert at all times.
2. Never throw implements during training unless a teacher or a coach is present.
3. Keep behind the throwing area until everyone has thrown.
4. Do not fetch implements until instructed to do so by a teacher or coach.
5. Never engage in horseplay during training or competition.

Throwing Events

The throwing events give an opportunity for people who are bigger to take part in an exciting and satisfying activity. In all the throws, the implement must land inside a **designated** area in order for the throw to be measured. Each competitor gets three or six throws, with the best one counting.

The shot put

A shot is a metal ball that the competitor, using one hand, pushes away from a position against the side of the neck. This pushing action is known as putting and gives the event its name.

The shot is put from a throwing circle. The competitor starts at the rear of the circle, facing the opposite way from the direction the shot is to be thrown. In one smooth action, the shot putter glides backwards across the circle with the back leg bent. When the athlete hits the wooden **stop board** at the throwing side of the circle, it is time to turn around, straighten the leg, and propel the shot on its way. If the competitor steps outside the circle while throwing or in the **follow through** then the throw is disqualified. A competition shot can weigh from 8 pounds to 16 pounds.

Judy Oakes, British champion, releases the shot in perfect style.

The discus

The discus is saucer-shaped and made of wood with a metal edging. The start position is similar to the shot put with the competitor standing at the back of the throwing circle.

TRACK AND FIELD FACTS

The throwing circle diameter

Shot put	7 feet
Discus	8 feet
Hammer	7 feet

Holding the discus in one hand, the thrower takes a few swings of the throwing arm and then crosses the circle holding the arm behind while spinning around to gain **momentum**. When the leading foot hits the front of the circle, the discus is released with a sweeping sidearm motion. A discus can weigh from 2 pounds, 3 ounces to 4 pounds, 6 ounces.

The hammer

The hammer is a metal ball attached to a handle by a steel wire. The implement has an overall length of about 47 inches. Similar to the shot put event, hammer throwing starts from inside a caged circle. The hammer is held with both hands on the handle. After taking a few practice swings of the hammer, the competitor rotates across the circle. At the front of the circle, the hammer is released with the arms outstretched. The hammer weighs 16 pounds. Women use a lighter hammer.

The javelin

The javelin is a sharpened spear made of metal. The thrower holds the javelin in one hand at shoulder height while building up speed by running down a marked runway. During the last few strides the javelin is pulled back with the arm fully extended. As the front foot hits the ground for the last time before the throw, the athlete brakes. The power and speed are then transferred through the body to the javelin.

Learning
the javelin.
The young
athlete
follows
through.

Relay Racing

Relay races are the only track and field events in which a team competes in one event. The different combinations of talents and skills make relay races very exciting for the spectators and challenging for the competitors. In senior competitive track and field, there are two main relay races: the 4 by 100-meter relay and the 4 by 400-meter relay. In the first race, four teammates each run about 100 meters and in the second, four teammates each run 400 meters. Each of the four relays is called a **leg**. There are relay competitions for both men's and women's teams.

In a relay race, the team members run in turn, passing a **baton** from one runner to the next. This means that learning the technique of the baton change is very important. Four good sprinters with excellent baton changes can often beat a team made up of faster sprinters who haven't practiced their changeovers. There is an old saying in track and field that is still true today: "It's the speed of the baton that counts."

Members of a U.S. relay team execute a changeover. Note how both athletes are looking ahead and the outgoing sprinter's arm is outstretched.

The baton needs to pass from runner to runner at the fastest possible speed. This means that the outgoing runner has to know when to start sprinting so that the incoming runner can catch up and pass the baton while they are both in the 22-meter-long "changeover zone." Only with constant practice at full speed can the exact same changeover point be achieved time after time.

TRACK AND FIELD FACTS

The name given to the last leg of a relay race is the "anchor leg."

Dennis Mitchell leads the U.S. men's 4 by 100-meters relay team in the 1996 Atlanta Olympic Games.

A mark can be placed on the track so the outgoing runner will know that when the mark is passed by the incoming runner it is time to set off. The outgoing runner does not look back but runs a few strides and then confidently places a steady and straight arm out behind to grab the baton. After the changeover is completed, the runner immediately changes the baton to the other hand. If it is the last leg of the race, then the baton can stay in the same hand.

In the 4 by 400-meters relay, in which each leg of the race is one lap of the track, the changeover is complicated by the fact that the racers do not need to stay in their own lanes after the first lap and a quarter. This means that both the incoming and outgoing runners must be sure that the handover is not ruined by crowding in the lane. Instead of looking ahead, the outgoing runner looks back, almost until the moment of the changeover, to make sure that the changeover is going smoothly. In a race this long, the speed of the pass becomes less important than its reliability.

In addition to the competition relays, there are other relay races especially for younger athletes. These are known as "shuttle relays." In a shuttle, the runners line up at the start and finish of a sprint race distance, and change over with their teammates by tapping them on the shoulder.

Getting Started

Most young people interested in sports can begin training and competing in track and field while they are still at school. If they are talented, they may have a chance to compete against other schools in their town or region. If they are very good they may have a chance to run, jump, and throw in state and district high-school meets. Many Olympic and world champions have started out this way.

An important thing for a young athlete to remember is not to specialize in any one event too early. There are numerous examples of top world athletes who have begun their athletics careers in one event only to discover that their real talent was in another event.

Many countries, including the United States, organize international competitions for the best junior athletes. Anyone under twenty can compete as a junior. The World Junior Championships are held every other year.

The 20-kilometer walk at the World Championships in Stuttgart.

If a junior athlete continues at the senior level, there are many opportunities for competitions. Many athletes compete at the college level in regional, state, and national meets. In the United States, the National Collegiate Athletic Association (NCAA) and the National Association of Intercollegiate Athletics (NAIA) run college championships. Anyone can compete in an open meet, and some organizations sponsor invitational meets, that only invited athletes may enter.

The best-known of the major international competitions are the Olympic Games and the World Championships. The World Championships were first held in 1983 at Helsinki, Finland. This competition is now held every two years. For special groups of countries there are also the European Championships, the Commonwealth Games, and the Pan American Games. Like the Olympic Games, all of these are held every four years. There are also two important **cup competitions**: the European Cup, which takes place every year, and the World Cup, which is held every four years.

Although track and field was once 99 percent an **amateur** sport, today many world-class performers are **professional** athletes and can get paid large sponsorship and appearance fees. For all young athletes there is a clear path that can lead the dedicated and talented to the top of the sport.

Track and Field Highlights

Track and field competes with soccer as the most popular and widespread sport in the world. The governing body is the International Amateur Athletic Federation (IAAF), which has 204 member countries. Individual countries have their own organizations governing the sport.

Over the years track and field has provided the sporting world with some great performances and personalities. In the period leading up to World War II, the leading U.S. athlete was the runner and jumper Jesse Owens. In 1936 at the Berlin Olympics, this African American won four gold medals. Adolf Hitler, the German Nazi leader, believed in the supremacy of the white race, and was very angry at Owens's success. No other track and field athlete won four gold medals at one Olympic Games until 1984, when another African American, Carl Lewis, won four golds at Los Angeles.

At the 1996 Olympic Games, Michael Johnson became the first man in Olympic history to win both the 200 meters and the 400 meters. He set a world record of 19.32 seconds in the 200 meters.

One of the greatest sporting achievements of the 20th century was the first running of a mile in under four minutes. Medical student Roger Bannister, running at Oxford, in England, made this breakthrough in 1954. His record was broken again only 42 days later.

Today, the sprinting events seem to attract the most attention. During the late 1970s and early 1980s, it was the middle distance running events that dominated the sport. The world records and Olympic medals won by such athletes as Sebastian Coe, Steve Ovett, and Steve Cram of Great Britain were front page news. Coe's world record for the 800 meters, which he set in 1981, still stood in 1996.

The women's sprint record set by American Florence Griffith Joyner in 1988 also still stood in 1996. Her time of 10.49 seconds for the 100 meters and 21.34 seconds for the 200 meters would beat the best men's record in some countries.

At the 1952 Olympics, a husband and wife each won gold medals. The Czech runner Emil Zatopek won three gold medals in the 5,000 meters, the 10,000 meters, and the marathon. His wife, Dana, won a gold in the women's javelin event the same day her husband won the 5,000 meters. Since 1983 women athletes have been able to compete in championship marathons. The fastest woman marathoner, Ingrid Kristiansen of Norway, with a time of 2:21:06, has run faster than Zatopek did in winning the gold at the 1952 Olympics.

Michael Johnson of the United States made track and field history in 1995 by becoming the first man in the 1900s to win the 200 meters and the 400 meters in a single meet. He repeated this feat twice that year—at both the U.S. and world championships.

Florence Griffith Joyner's 1988 sprint record has yet to be beaten.

Famous Faces

As athletes become more fit and the equipment, from the shoes to the track surface, changes, world records never seem to stand for more than two or three months, let alone two or three years. One exception to this trend was the almost unbelievable record held by the famous long-jumper Bob Beamon. At the 1968 Olympic Games in Mexico City, this tall American shocked the world and himself when he jumped the incredible distance of 29 feet, $2\frac{1}{2}$ inches. This beat the previous world record by an enormous $21\frac{1}{2}$ inches. Beamon's name appeared in the record books for more than 20 years before American Mike Powell beat it in Tokyo in 1991 with a jump of 29 feet, $4\frac{1}{2}$ inches.

Linford Christie, of Great Britain, one of the greatest sprinters of all time, has won many major titles, including Olympic, World, European, and Commonwealth. Born in Jamaica in 1960, Christie went to Britain when he was eight years old. He won his first major title in 1986—the European Indoor 200-meters sprint. In 1989 Christie was appointed British men's team captain. Currently the only European athlete ever to run 100 meters in under ten seconds, Christie was honored by his home borough, when the West London Stadium was renamed the Linford Christie Stadium.

Sally Gunnell, of Great Britain, is the world record holder for the 400-meter hurdles.

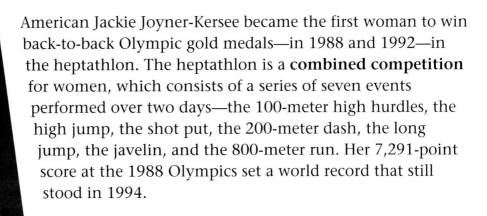

American Jackie Joyner-Kersee became the first woman to win back-to-back Olympic gold medals—in 1988 and 1992—in the heptathlon. The heptathlon is a **combined competition** for women, which consists of a series of seven events performed over two days—the 100-meter high hurdles, the high jump, the shot put, the 200-meter dash, the long jump, the javelin, and the 800-meter run. Her 7,291-point score at the 1988 Olympics set a world record that still stood in 1994.

Born in 1962, in East St. Louis, Illinois, Joyner-Kersee became a volleyball and basketball star in high school and set a state long jump record. She discovered the sport that would make her famous in college at the University of California at Los Angeles (UCLA) with the help of her coach, Bob Kersee, who would become her husband in 1986. Joyner-Kersee is also the sister-in-law of sprinting superstar Florence Griffith Joyner.

American Carl Lewis is probably the greatest sprinter of all time. He has also used his great speed and concentration to win four Olympic long jump titles. He first made an impact on the international scene at the World Championships of 1983, where he won three gold medals (100 meters, long jump, and relay). A year later, in front of his home crowd in Los Angeles, he won all three again, adding another gold in the 200 meters. In 1991 Lewis won what many consider to have been the greatest 100-meter race ever at the World Championships in Tokyo, setting a world record. Born in Birmingham, Alabama, in 1961, from 1981 to 1991, Lewis won 65 long jump competitions in a row. He also has run the 100 meters in under ten seconds fifteen times.

The greatest pole vaulter of all time is perhaps Sergei Bubka of Ukraine. He holds the world indoor and outdoor records and has won all the World Championships.

Glossary

amateur a sportsperson who receives no money for competing.

approach run the run up taken by an athlete before a jump or javelin throw.

attempt a try at doing something in competition.

baton the cylindrical-shaped object that relay racers pass from one to another.

cinder a coal by-product that running tracks used to be made of.

combined competition an event in which an athlete competes in a series of events. The pentathlon, the heptathlon, and the decathlon are combined competitions.

crouch start the position that the runners take before the start of a sprint.

designated the place where something or someone must go.

disqualified being barred from competing in any sport, by breaking the rules.

facilities the equipment and place where track and field events take place.

field the area encircled by the track where all the field events are held.

follow through the continuing movement of the athlete's body after an implement has been thrown.

fouling what happens in jumps and throws when the athlete goes in front of the circle, stop line, or take-off board.

implements things that are thrown in athletics, such as the shot, hammer, javelin, and discus.

invalid not allowed, disqualified.

leading the word used to describe the arm or leg that is in front or swinging forward as an athlete moves.

leg the part of the race run by one of the four team members.

limber flexible and easy to bend.

meet a track and field competition.

momentum force or speed caused by movement.

Olympic Games international sporting competition held at a different location every four years. Winter and summer games are held. Track and field is part of the summer Olympics.

pace judgment being able to judge what the speed is in a race.

pentathlon five-event competition, now replaced by the seven-event heptathlon for women.

professional a sportsperson who receives money to compete.

relays races that involve teams of four competing over given distances.

sprints races in which speed is the most important factor, such as the 100-meter race, 200-meter race, and 400-meter race.

stadium an arena with spectator seating especially constructed for sporting events.

staggered a start in which runners stand at various distances back, to ensure every runner covers the same distance on a track that has curves.

stamina the power required to continue even when an athlete is tired.

starting block a wedge-shaped object used to hold the foot or feet at a heel-up angle while a racer is in the start position.

stop board a board used in shot put to help stop forward momentum.

straight the straight part of an oval-shaped track. Each oval track has two straights.

synthetic material that is manufactured, not natural.

tactics mental abilities or strategy used to perform an event, such as distance races, high jump, or pole vault.

take-off board a wooden board used for the long jump and triple jump. If the athlete goes beyond the board, a foul is committed.

technique the method and skill used in performing an event.

tension mental and emotional strain.

track the oval-shaped running surface that encircles the field.

trailing word used in hurdling to describe the leg that is behind or swinging back as an athlete moves.

Index